Errol!

Zanni Louise & Philip Bunting

Come, Errol.

Errol?

Errol, come this very minute.

Errol, I'm going to count to three.

One ...

Errol, I've had it up to here!

Errol!

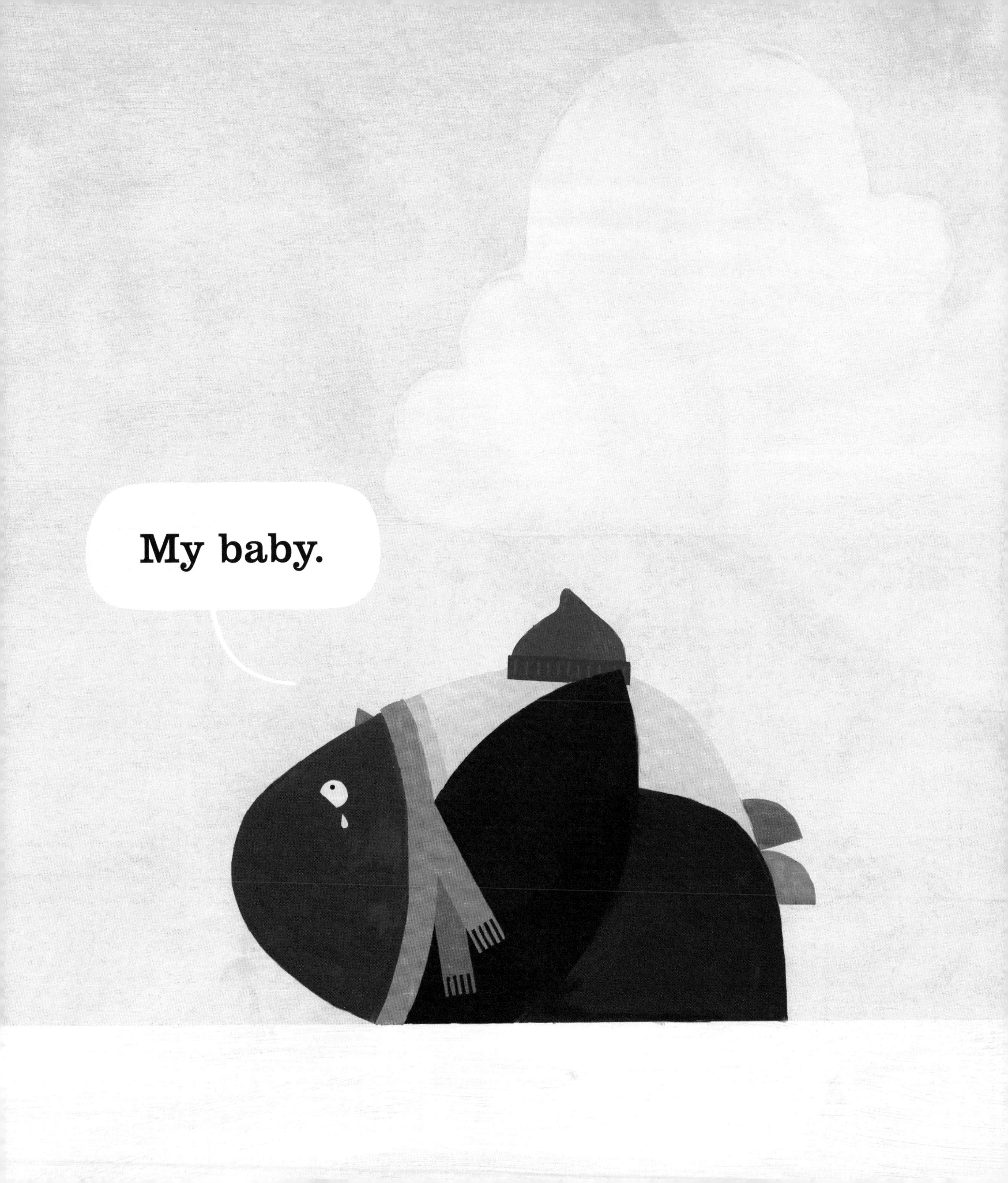
My baby.

Come, Mum.

Mum, come this very minute.

I'm going to count to three.

One. Two ...